TATTLE TALE
TALK # 1

FRANCIS M. EDWARDS

DEDICATION

This book is dedicated to the people who had faith in
me along the way, especially
My family
And
The unconditional love my doggies provided.

CONTENTS

ACKNOWLEDGMENTS

I wish to thank my English Professor at The University of Pittsburgh for telling me that I should write books. I will never forget his recommendation. You can do it attitude came from my English grandmother who was always there for me. Thanks to my extended family for their support.
I wrote this story from memory along with a fictitious imagination. I used no names or made up names to protect the innocent.

1 FALSE IMPRESSIONS

Come on…find the clues and figure out the answers then save your industrious work. Submit all QUESTION SHEETS from each book in the series of three books to find out if you are the one who correctly answered the questions and is picked to be the contest winner. Each of three books contains ten questions The PRIZE: MY FAMILY HOME. Please read all the details of this contest on the Details Page.

This will be my legacy to give someone a beautiful home. The American Dream has been slipping away for too many people in our nation.

What was one to think moving to a place proclaiming "Entering Kennebunkport" … and not "Welcome To", as most towns do on there greeting signs? I should have known not to trust twenty-five years of my life to living in such a place, but everything that wasn't sold in New Jersey and all the possessions my family could not part with sat in the first of fifteen trucks of household goods outside the real estate office on a very cold January day.

We did look at various possibilities on a few trips to Maine, but everything was sold or under contract by the time we could make our move. The only option left to us was a residential house called Heartbreak Hotel. A local restaurateur had owned the house and had rented out the rooms to anyone who needed a place to sleep for a few bucks. When each summer came to an end, the boys and girls separated returning to college or to wherever, and thus the name stuck with the local townspeople.

Sitting in New Jersey, Maine became an illusion gathered on one's mind from looking at all the picture calendars, magazines, and books depicting an idealistic way of life. White clapboard houses with green shutters on peaceful elm treed lined streets near rocky beaches with picture perfect blue sky and ocean. An inert feeling of embracing Colonial America in Maine appealed to one's sense of longing for a simple and uncomplicated life. After all, my uncle assessed the only choice we had by proclaiming; "One could not find a better situated house in America with a barn that overlooked the main business area of a town".

We only had the information from the listing sheet that we took back to New Jersey, when we made the decision to purchase the house. I can only remember stopping in front of the house on one of our trips to view properties. I went up onto the front porch and lost interest at first sight, when I saw the peeling white paint on the clapboard siding and rotten floorboards on the porch. The house was situated only about five feet from the street, so I guessed that this was done so that one would not have much snow to shovel in order to get out into the street. This house just had no curb appeal even though; it had a four-story barn attached to the backside of the house. We learned at the closing that the furnace might not be working, since all the radiators froze up and burst when the water thawed. The real estate agent told us that the real former owner who was the last person in her family line was 100 years old and confined to a nursing home had heard that a family was purchasing the home. She was just delighted to hear the news. We were only the fourth owner of the home, since it was built in 1745.

Our illusion was quickly shattered as the reality of our situation became more apparent upon our arrival at the house. The house was unlivable. We quickly rented a seaside cottage for 6 weeks, while we drew up a plan of attack. The real estate agent informed us that we had to hire the local boys to do any work if we wanted to "fit into the fabric of the town". We had no objection to this scheme and made the necessary telephone calls to arrange help. The local telephone operator at the other end of the line overheard all those calls. We paid for a private telephone line, but all lines in the town somehow were third party! We didn't mind this as this was a way of broadcasting that we were going to be good neighbors and hire only local boys to do such work as scrapping and painting the clapboard siding. Architecturally speaking, the style of the house was called Greek Revival with the distinguishing end columns. The painters found traces of black paint along the stripes of the columns. The decision was made to paint those black for a complete original restoration of how the house looked around the Civil War in 1860 when the house was first painted. Before that time, we learned that the houses in the town remained natural in their cedar raw wood color. The black painted stripes were complemented with black shutters. This restoration scheme caused quite a stir within the town. We did not conform to the norm of an all white house with green shutters, which are found in most New England towns. This painting scheme had its origins after War World 11 to left the spirits and ends the doldrums of war. People sent us old photographs of New England houses painted with black trim to support our cause but this was to no avail. The local folks just didn't like what we did referring to the house as "pin-stripe". Someone even gave us an old photograph of our house with the black trim, metal roof and granite fence that ran along the front of the house. We learned that some Boston builders purchased a lot of the granite fences in New England towns in order to use the stone in their construction of bank buildings in Boston.   The photo showed a horse and carriage leaving the barn. This gave us the idea to call our new house, The Carriage House.

The local post office in Kennebunkport never delivered mail to a property. Everyone had to go to the post office to collect mail at a post office box. This arrangement assured that all the local gossip slipped from one ear to another.   Rumor flew about one of the painters we hired. The town folk wanted us to know that one of them one night went on a drug binge, returned home and broke a window entering his sister's bedroom to molest and ravage her. Somehow, I never could bring myself to believe that story, even though the other painters never let that handsome sixteen-year-old boy on a ladder to scrape the old peeling paint off the house. I guess he was always too high to be on a ladder two stories up. One day he confirmed the gossip about himself, but he told me that he never remembered doing anything so bad as the rumor proclaimed.

A few days later I attended his memorial service with another two hundred people at The South Congregational Church; he stood in front of a fast moving freight train.

One day after leaving our rented cottage, we heard a car honking at us. It turned out to be some neighbors from New Jersey. These people noticed my rusty blue van and connected it with us. We told them that we were looking for a food store to buy provisions.

They directed us to a food store 25 miles inland to a city called Sanford. They told us that was the nearest food store. I started to get concerned for my family and wondered how one could live here in the winter. I guess we needed to invest in a large freezer to make sure provisions would be handy for those snowed in situations. Actually, maybe those people were playing a joke on us, because there was a super market about 10 miles from Kennebunkport in another town called Saco.

The Carriage House had no kitchen to speak of; it was located in the area that connected the house to the barn. It consisted of a rough passage room with no cabinets, an old sink and an old chimney that once had a potbelly stove or something connected to it. One had too walk through a narrow hallway from the dining room; turn left and step down a step to get into the kitchen room. Matters even got more complicated, because the only bathroom in the house was located above the kitchen in another passageway to the second floor of the barn with the same handicap entrance as the kitchen. This bathroom had a white porcelain claw footed tub, pedestal sink and a toilet. Maybe the former owner thought the necessity of a bathroom should be located away from the living area of the house for sanitary reasons when the decision was made to bring plumbing indoors. Another dozen rooms made up the main house. The whole house needed a complete renovation; oak floors sanded, walls re-wallpapered, trim painted, ceilings patched and wallpapered, new baseboard heating, re-wired and a new roof. Those improvements were the basics to make the house livable, which included mapping out new bathrooms that could be located between bedrooms and a new kitchen that involved a work permit from the local planning board. This was turned thumbs down. "A lot of people have their kitchens located far away from their dining rooms in passage ways to their barns. This is very normal in New England. A lot of out of townies want to come here and change things." I really think that the variance committee just wanted to punish us for the black trim.

Our basic game plan was to renovate one room at a time and then call New Jersey to send up another truck full of furniture for the renovated room. I was suppose to go back to New Jersey and continue with my employment at the Golden Nugget Casino in Atlantic City which was only 10 miles from Ocean City. I just could not leave Maine with all the work that was required to restore the house to livable conditions for my family members.

The casinos and the crime they festered was one of the major reasons for seeking out a tranquil existence in Maine. I was working the graveyard shift in the coin department of the casino. We heard lots of horror stories of casino patrons being followed home and then robbed of their winnings. Prostitutes claimed their territory on every corner of Atlantic City and would actually come up to you and grope your private parts. Like many of the established families in Ocean City, we joined them in offering our house for sale. An investor purchased our homestead giving us a year to move, since he wasn't going to tear down our house right away. This created a perfect situation for us, since we needed everything we could possibly scrape form our home to move to Maine including the kitchen sink.

I even took the wallpaper. There were no stores near Kennebunkport that supplied building materials. We had to travel to Massachusetts from Maine to find such stores except for one local hardware store whose owner was a selectman. Again, we all received the silent message that we needed to support the local merchants in our town whenever possible to be good citizens.

The Carriage House is not only situated overlooking Dock Square business area but also is directly down the street facing The South Congregational Church.   This church is reported to be one of the most photographed churches in New England with its noted Greek revival columns and large clock tower. Congregational means interdenominational, local community oriented serving all needs. The minister is the head of the church and makes all decisions that needed to be made in order to run his church.   Directly across the street from The Carriage House and starting from the corner down towards Dock Square is zoned commercial. On the other side of the corner going north is zoned Village Residential including my side of the street. Village Residential allowed the creation of a limited commercial business on the property with the planning board's permission. We received permission to have an antiques shop in the barn. We needed this for our overflow of stuff from New Jersey that just looked out of place in our Colonial Home. Victorian antiques looked too modern and overbearing, so we were glad to sell them off achieving the "right" look.

The barn on our property was three stories high with a cupola that provided a view of the river that came up from the ocean about a mile away. Wives of sea captains and seamen would look out from the cupola searching for a glimpse of a ship's mast to see if their husbands were coming up the river in the 1800's.

Captain Mason, who traded in salt, built the Carriage House in 1745. This was before the American Revolution, and if your chimney was painted white you showed loyalty to the King of England, and therefore British solders would not burn down your house. If on the other hand, you left your chimney natural red brick you remained loyal to the Yankee rebels. The Crown owned all the large the trees in New England. A colonist was only allowed to cut a tree down to use in the construction of their buildings only if the diameter of the tree was less than 23 inches wide. I measured the wallboards exposed in our barn and they all were just slightly less than 23 inches wide. If the Crown found wider boards in your home, you would be hanged in the town square. The Crown needed all the larger trees in New England to build hulls for their new ships. Most of the British Naval Fleet was built in New England towns like Kennebunkport, Maine. Old photographs show many ship builders headquarters or huts alongside the river beside The South Congregational Church.

Shipbuilding was a major industry that kept the town thriving well into the late 1800's. Many whaling ships and fishing ships found their way into the Atlantic Ocean and around the world from shipbuilders in the Kennebunks.

These shipbuilders exercised their skills in building oversized and stately looking homes all along the Kennebunk River for themselves and wealthy ship captains. Each house has its own distinctive style and appeal hidden behind large elm trees. Many of those houses have window shutters that can be recessed into the wall or be pulled out in order to act as barriers from Indian arrows. This is probably the origin of window shutters in New England. The shutter was modified over the years only to be added to a house for "looks".

Indian tribes used to come to Kennebunkport from as far away as Canada in the summertime to hunt and fish. They co-existed with the colonists most of the time. However, there are accounts by authors who describe Indians from Quebec, Canada who raided the town and kidnapped women to take them back to Canada. The cottage owner that we rented from told me that her great grandmother was shot by an Indian arrow and died on her way home from The South Congregational Church one Sunday. I believe the Indians came to the town for the summer as late as the 1930's.

The Carriage House and surrounding buildings all seemed to have many windows with 12 panes of glass in each window. In fact, The Carriage House had windows in places for no apparent practical reason at all. Some windows were closed up with shutters that had solid walls behind the windows. I learned that the Crown in Colonial times taxed each windowpane. The more windowpanes a property had the more prestige the family could claim.

Our motives for moving to Kennebunkport, Maine soon became blurred as we took on the new task of restoring the home room by room.

2 TRADEGY

No family is immune to tragedy and disappointments. One day a call came from New Jersey to relay the information that my sister had cervical cancer and had to be treated soon. Health insurance wasn't an option we could rely upon. Doctors told us The National Institute of Health (NIH) in Washington D. C. was looking for just 10 patients who had certain stages of the disease and if qualified could be admitted free. My sister was one of one thousand interviewed for their program. This meant that I had to stay in Maine to free up our van for trips to NIH from New Jersey. This news circulated around our small town. One day I noticed a truck parked in the courtyard area in front of the barn with a note attached to the windshield, "Please feel free to use this transportation." It was wonderful to have wheels to get supplies and food. Someone in the town really cared about my plight.

My aunt and my other sister made many trips to D. C. taking my sick sister for treatment. On one occasion they had to stay over and checked into the local motel that was recommended to them by NIH. The room was crawling with bed bugs. They quickly left the place and got a room at The Marriott and took a swim in their pool. The ladies wanted something to drink, but the soda machine was not working. A man with a clipboard was walking along the pool area, and the ladies asked, "Do you work here? Could we order some refreshments?" Later, they heard a knock at their door and a hotel employee delivered a tray full of drinks and sandwiches with a note: "Compliments from The Hotel President... yes I do work here". The next morning my aunt entered the candy shop to purchase some goodies and noticed some empty boxes, asking if she could take them. Just as she was walking out of the shop The Hotel President saw her and asked what she was doing with those empty boxes? She replied that she was moving to Maine and leaving society. He replied, "In that case, society will move to Maine"!

Summer was coming soon. The renovation and in particular the outside painting was going too slow. I got so sick of hearing the scraping day after day for weeks on end that one day I stormed out of the house and told those local boys to put their scrapers away and start painting or I would refuse to pay them any more money. They scraped just the front of the house and front of the barn for six whole weeks. By the time the front of the house and barn received a primer and finish coat of paint I ran out of money. The rest of the house never did get painted for another eight years, but the good news was that really no one could see the rest of the house and barn for all the trees. I had hoped that our neighbors had gotten use to seeing the pealing paint. None of them said anything to me. Those local boys received six thousand dollars for painting half a house! I needed to conserve the family cash as best I could in order to supply necessary cash for my family and their trips to D.C.

Everyone in my family decided to visit me and spend Memorial Weekend in Kennebunkport. My family members consisted of my aunt, uncle, and two sisters, not forgetting Muffy our collie dog. My aunt and uncle who are sister and brother never married.

They raised my brother, and my two sisters, and me from childhood when their sister, my mother, passed away. My brother was the only one of us who lived on his own with his wife and four children in Pittsburgh, Pennsylvania.

This was going to be quite an occasion with a fitting house warming party. The Kennebunkport Memorial Day Parade was going to go right past The Carriage House. We would be able to have a front row seat to view the high school marching band and distinguished Veterans marching down towards Dock Square. They place a wreath in the Kennebunk River in remembrance of all those brave men and women who sacrificed their life for our country. I decorated our now painted house with red, white, and blue bunting and hosted an American Flag on a sailboat mast that I found in the barn. Upon hearing the patriotic music coming down the street, we all assembled on the second floor porch to view the procession. Just as the marching band reached our house, we heard a loud cracking sound. Our porch collapsed as on lookers screamed in horror to warn spectators to run off the first floor porch. No one got hurt, but we gingerly crept off the porch and into the doorway one at a time. Of course, this made the local newspaper with picture. We stole the show.

After this calamity, everyone returned to New Jersey or Pennsylvania. Muffy and me settled down to finishing the house and running the antiques or second hand business. My sister continued her treatments in D.C.

One of our neighbors, who lived behind our house in New Jersey, was a former jewelry storeowner. He offered to keep the family jewelry in a safe place until my sister's treatment ended. One day he came rushing over to our house to ask how we acquired one diamond ring in particular? My aunt explained that it was purchased for her mother who had sold her ring in the Great Depression and could only replace her wedding ring with imitation diamond rings bought from Five and Dime stores. My aunt wanted her mother to have a real diamond. My aunt asked our local jeweler at the time for the biggest diamond ring that six hundred dollars could buy. Our neighbor said, he has seen very "few flawless diamond stones, 1 ct. in weight". When my grandmother passed away, the ring was given to my sick sister to wear. It needed to be resized to fit her finger, so she took the ring to a jeweler. I just could not believe that the stone was worth anything more than what was paid for it. Many years later, my sister decided that it was time to give the ring to my other sister to wear. We took it to another friend jeweler, this time in Kittery, Maine who refused to size the ring for my sister. He said, the ring belongs to my aunt. "As long as you keep this ring, you will always have your family to take care of you". He confirmed what the other jeweler had documented about the stone. After much thought, the only plausible explanation for this good fortune was that my sick sister received a different ring than the one she dropped off for sizing so many yeas ago.

During my first summer in Maine, I became especially friendly with a local restaurant owner who introduced me to a lobster club sandwich. This unusual delicacy was unique to her restaurant. I use to walk down to her restaurant on the river with Muffy every evening for that delicious lobster club sandwich. Muffy would stay outside in the parking lot behind the restaurant and have meals that were compliments of the owner. One day, after I finished my meal inside, Muffy was gone. I learned that a car had backed up over her. This probably scared the wits out of her as she ran the entire way home unhurt. This was my sick sister's beautiful sable collie dog. I wanted to protect and preserve this pet for my sister. I took her for a swim every morning for her exercise. She would just bark and bark her head off with happiness as she paddled out to retrieve a thrown stick. I thought Muffy was not suffering from any separation anxiety from the family, until I came to renovate the last room in The Carriage House.

Three days before Labor Day Weekend I received a phone call from my family that they were all finally returning to Kennebunkport to settle in and live. My sister was cured! The doctors at NIH could not see the tumor nor feel the tumor. They decided that double dosing the radiation treatment at the last minute would insure that the cancer would never reappear and her life would be saved. This procedure would be recorded in medical journals as an advanced way to treating cervical cancer. After fifty-nine pap smears and dozens of doctors

who were involved in this study, all concluded
that finally my sister could be released from
their care. She could move to Maine.

The only problem I had was that I had no
assurance that my sister could ever sleep in the
bedroom that she had picked out in The
Carriage House. I had stored all her
furnishings in the second floor of the barn when
the last truckload arrived in Maine. I just could
never bring myself to ever going into her room.
The idea to redecorate and fix up her room
saddened me too much, because I thought that
she would never overcome her problem to see
or enjoy it.   However, somehow Muffy always
found herself to my sister's room and defecated
dozens of time on the floor during the summer.
How could this happen? I was always with
Muffy in a different area of the house. I could
not smell the problem, but I was astonished to
find the problem when I checked out her room
to list what it would take to refurbish the room

before my sister's arrival. I forgave Muffy and scoured the room.

I told the restaurateur about the good news that I received from my family, and my agonizing news that my sister's room wasn't ready. Soon dozens of the local towns people showed up at my front door with paintbrushes in hand, wallpaper, rolls of carpet, window shades, curtains and the right color of paint that my sister had picked out at the local hardware store months ago. Work went on for two days. The room was finished when I saw my sister's bed being carried out of the barn and placed in her room. I was so grateful to all those local townspeople who took my family to heart and made my sister's bedroom ready for her arrival. Another surprise was waiting for all of us; a full course Maine lobster dinner was given in celebration, compliments from my friend the restaurateur.

Fall in New England is a particular beautiful time of year as the various trees show their blazing colors of red and yellow. This is also the time of year when people like me wonder what to do in order to survive, once the tourists leave at the end of October. I decided to take the real estate course and become a broker. I asked the town fathers to grant me a change of use for the barn from antiques to office. I got the change and became the only real estate office in Kennebunkport, a town of only three thousand people and less in the winter.

The whole family was looking forward to our first Christmas in Maine. The beautiful pictures of New England during the Christmas season conjured up loving images of fresh pine wreaths with red bows fasten to white clapboard homes decorated with white lights reflecting the fresh fallen snow sparking like diamonds. This was far from the reality in

Kennebunkport. The Carriage House was the only house that had a pine wreath with red ribbon displayed on the front door. The only truth in the picture was the snow that had fallen a few days before Christmas. This was just too much for my family to accept, so they encouraged me to set up a meeting with the few businesses that remained open during the wintertime. We businessmen tossed around many ideas. I suggested that we just promote Christmas as it comes around every year. Everyone voted on my idea and came up with a unanimous decision to promote Kennebunkport at Christmas. If you look at any of the promotional literature, you will soon find that I am never given any credit for inventing the event the town calls Prelude. Prelude would take place the first weekend of every December. This event would include and promote all the local charities as well as businesses. This idea extended the tourist season from summer into late fall by keeping all the local businesses open. The weather for the first Prelude was unnaturally warm around 70 degrees and thousands of people descended on Kennebunkport to enjoy all the festivities. The businesses' cash registers rang up sales sounding like bells pealing the good news of Christ's birth. Thus, a tradition was born that continues to this day with Santa Clause arriving via lobster boat on the Kennebunk River, landing in Dock Square.

However, during our first Christmas in Kennebunkport, we sought out Portland, Maine for festive cheering by attending a Christmas concert given by the Portland Symphony. My sister could not manage to sit in her seat without getting up every few minutes. "What's wrong"? "I have a pain in my back," she said. The next day, a call was made to NIH and, we were informed to bring her back to their hospital for a chemotherapy treatment.

A Loss

So Sad

Beauty Lost

Dreams Gone

Aspirations Done

Sorrow Looms

Fate Pokes

End Covers

Until Woken

AT HOPE

Once again, my sister was released to return to Maine. This time her stomach just kept getting bigger and bigger with pain increasing daily. We heard that chemotherapy treatment either cures you or kills you. God called her to his side at 36 years of age on a frigid February day from her own bedroom in The Carriage House

Our family burial plots are in Pittsburgh, Pennsylvania. My sister's love for Maine persuaded us to make arrangements, so that she could be interred at our local cemetery called "Hope". None of my family realized that during those winter months in Maine, bodies are kept in small huts along the side of the road until the spring thaw. Funerals are done a second time along side the permanent gravesite in the cemetery. My family decided that we could not go through two funerals. We would fly her to Pittsburgh. However, the local funeral home director said, that he would "twist arms and do one funeral here in Maine with interment in the ground". This news made headliners and good post office gossip. The cemetery keeper was on vacation in Florida and flown back to Maine to bulldoze a path to the plot located on the Kennebunkport side of the cemetery. We heard that the snow was six feet deep and dynamite was used to blast out frozen rock in order to have a vault fitted inside the hole to accommodate a coffin.

We didn't need a viewing room at the funeral home, because only a very few people personally knew our family. No wake was needed, but members of my family wanted to say a last good-bye, so they made their way to the funeral home to find my sister lying in state in a garage. The minister and his helper at The South Congregational Church accommodated my family with Episcopal paraphernalia to make the church service as comfortable as possible for us, including the use of The Common

Prayer Book. The minister was very understanding and conducted an Episcopal Funeral Service both inside the church and at the gravesite lost in mounds of snowdrifts. After the funeral, my brother's wife asked to have some mementos in remembrance of my sister to take back to Pittsburgh. I was gracious and complied with those wishes by placing several sterling silver items on the chest of drawers in her bedroom. When my brother's family left Kennebunkport for their home I found a note along with the silver items. "I wanted the diamond ring."

Mud Season came to Kennebunkport in March, when the ground thawed giving us an opportunity to place a headstone upon my sister's grave. My uncle with my help went into the cemetery to pour a concrete base for a white marble bench purchased on a side trip to a Vermont marble mine. A day later, we went back to see if the cement had harden and found a note attached to the foundation that read, "Call the cemetery keeper". Embarrassed and apologetic that we maybe should have not intruded upon the cemetery by the way we conducted ourselves, the keeper said, "You placed the foundation in the wrong spot. We had to move your sister because she was in the wrong place. Remember all the snow?" I said, "Yes, and please just move our cement foundation to the right place for us, thanks. We have a marble bench to place on the foundation." My family purchased six cemetery plots (three plots in front of another three plots); therefore we wanted the marble bench to be placed in the middle of the plots. To this day, I am not sure exactly which grave my sister is resting in. I know that she is in the Kennebunkport side of the cemetery in good company with such notable people as the Walkers.

3.Daily Bread

The real estate office opened, but I realized that to sustain my family in the future, we needed a daily cash cow. Two doors away from The Carriage House, a home came on the market for sale. It was a Victorian home with seven bedrooms that would make a perfect bed and breakfast. I spoke to our town's building inspector, and he said that as long as the property has one parking space for each bedroom there should be no problem as this use is allowed in the Village Residential Zone.

He did mention that the selectmen were favoring a limit of only two rooms that could be rented in that zone come March and the spring vote. I had no worries about this zoning proposal, because this was November and therefore, I would be grand fathered by spring if the zoning change passed. The property was situated on a corner lot with lots of space surrounding the building.

The purchase of the property necessitated a trip to England to purchase English antique furnishings for the public rooms. Of course, New England has its British roots and English influences, so we thought to expound upon those realities with a whole container full of the finest English furniture for our Inn. We visited many antique shops and purchased fine old oak furniture. One very accommodating service a shipper provides is collecting all your purchases from the various shops that you purchased from, packing them together, and filling a container for ocean transportation. Once the container clears customs, the container arrives at your given address.

On one occasion a dealer in antiques asked me, "What do you personally like to collect"? I replied, "marine art". He told me about a painter who lived on a farm 250 miles north from where we were located. A few days later, on a very rainy day off we went to visit the painter. We ended up purchasing a wonderful historical maritime oil painting for our new Inn at a give away price of only a hundred dollars. The oil painting depicted Admiral Nelson's fleet returning home up the Thames River in London, after defeating Napoleon's warships. We gave a warm invitation to the painter to visit us in Maine to do research on the shipbuilding activities that took place in Kennebunkport.

My family made this trip to England as part vacation and part business. We all needed a break away to collect our thoughts and air out our hearts from the grieving that we all were consumed by in dealing with our family tragedy. It was during this trip that I began to understand the Englishness of my grandmother who raised me along with my three other siblings when her daughter passed away. It was my grandmother coupled with her son and daughter that made us a kinship bond. Even though we never understood many things my Nana talked about when I was young, I was now able to relate to those Victorian English traditions experiencing some of them first hand. For instance, the pantomime is a theatrical entertainment during the Christmas season suited for the whole family. It is filled with slapstick comedy and ridiculously funny situations during the performance of a children's fairy tale. Those performances are given in every town in England making them a major part of England's Christmas festivities. We don't have anything that comes close to this spellbinding experience. Another English tradition is the Christmas cracker. This is a table favor that has two ends that are pulled by you and your partner sitting next to you. This action makes a snap; opening up the cracker to reveal a paper hat and a small toy or trinket. Some stores offer Christmas crackers that sell for a few pounds to hundreds of pounds. The crackers are placed on the dinning table as part of the Christmas feast. The day after Christmas is a holiday in England called Boxing Day. I found many explanations for the day. Some English people think that the servants receive the day off to celebrate Christmas with their families and receive their bonuses. Others believe the holiday means taking a boxed lunch to a sporting event. Maybe the real reason lies in the practice of churches giving mite boxes or money to the poor. To this day their Queen always goes to church on Boxing Day and hands out tokens to the deserving. The modern idea for Boxing Day is the return of your Christmas gifts for exchange in the shops. Whatever the reason for the holiday, my own family members were never allowed to venture modern thought bends toward the idea of to their jobs on that particular day, even in America.

There are many foods that are associated with England that became part of my diet without me even knowing that their origins are indeed English. The trifle is a special dessert served at special occasions like birthdays and is made from custard, raspberry jam, and ladyfingers and topped with whipped cream. Other English food includes such mouth-watering temptations as plum pudding, mince pies, scones, hot pot, Shepherd's pie, roasted chestnuts, fish and chips, lemon cheese and bubble and squeak to name a few.

We always traveled to England on a very tight budget. One time we even cooked a turkey and took it along for food. We hung it out the hotel window in London to keep it cold. We eventually found a note attached to our room door asking us to remove the bird hanging from our window. You could see the turkey from the front street of the hotel. On other trips we would seek out the grocery stores to purchase lunchmeat and bread. We lived on sandwiches made by us in our hotel room.

We decided to call our new property an Inn and applied for a sign permit. The planning board didn't like the use of our word Inn. They decided that the word bed and breakfast should be used. We hired the local attorney to press our request to use the word Inn, since we were offering public rooms for our guests to use. We won this issue and received our permit. A fifteen hundred dollar hand carved wooden sign from solid mahogany was ordered from a local wood working man who also owned a local guesthouse. This handsome sign looked like a stern of a ship with the name, Port Gallery Inn, carved into solid mahogany wood on both sides. Once hanged on the supporting columns, we received a call from the town fathers, who claimed that our sign was too big! The poor woodworker had to take a buzz saw and cut here and there to reduce the size of the sign to a two square foot over all dimension from an oval shape (cost another five hundred dollars). When the town fathers saw the final product, they said nothing, because I guess it was better looking than the garbage can lid that I used to replace the original carved sign until the sign was adjusted in size.

All the other local bed and breakfasts were inquiring if we could be open for the town's Christmas Prelude. These establishments booked my inn and sent in reservations along with deposits for our grand opening. This was a very nice jester, and we certainly could use the money in November. The only problem was that we were just not ready to receive guests or friends. First, the wall coverings that were purchased in England ran short of what we needed to finish a room. The rooms were only half wallpapered, but wall-to-wall carpeting was installed. Second, the bedroom furniture that we ordered from North Carolina arrived only two days before Prelude in a snowstorm. The truck driver unloaded the furniture in the street saying, "This is where my liability ends". After hauling all the boxes into the first floor of the inn and unpacking all the furniture, we found only tops to twenty-five hutches with no bottoms, no headboards and no bed frames. We had planned to place a television in each of the seven hutches in the upper part while using the lower part for dresser drawers. We had no choice but to lay a box spring with a mattress directly on the floor (those were manufactured by a firm in the next town beside

Kennebunkport, called Biddeford). Our rooms looked quite sparse. Third, my uncle turned plumber insisted that he could use the large hallway on the second floor of the Inn to construct en suite bathrooms for four of the bedrooms. He promised all would be ready for Prelude. This fete required building walls, hanging doors, not to mention installing fixtures and sewer lines. Lastly, many friends including family got news of our grand opening. They all decided that it would be fun to experience Prelude festivities as they all made their journey to Kennebunkport. We always welcomed everyone. "The more the merrier", became our family slogan!

I instructed everyone to check in at the real estate office first, before venturing up to the Inn. The guests were encouraged to secure their restaurant dinner reservations for the weekend by walking around the town to the different establishments. Meanwhile, I can remember making a phone call up to the Inn to warn family and friends that were running around the Inn trying to hang curtains, hide boxes, paint buckets and cleaning up messes that our guests will be arriving soon. Word had gotten around to our few friends in town that we needed help at the Inn, so they pitched in as best they could to assist in getting beds made and equipped with linens, towels and soap. The first guests that I had sent around 5 p.m. to explore the town and make dinner reservations came back to the real estate office and requested their rooms. It was now around 9 p.m. and snowing very hard.

Once again I called the Inn to announce, "Ready or not here come our guests"! These first guests were two couples who came together to share their Prelude experiences with one another. I took them timidly and walked very slowly through the falling snow up to the Inn and into the back door. Just as we walked in front of the back circular stairs that maids use to use, my uncle tripped and fell down those stairs and landed at our feet. He was more embarrassed than hurt. I told the guests to just step over "the plumber" and proceed to the front reception area.

Somehow my uncle regained his composure and met me on the second floor and informed me what bathroom fixtures worked in each of the two rooms these guests were going to occupy.

Our guests heard him and they were stunned to find out that one toilet worked in one room and only one bathtub was functional in another. They insisted that they could not possibly tolerate this situation. Quickly, I interrupted their train of thought with declaring, "I am very glad that you know each other. I am sure if you act civil to each other that it would not be such a handicap to share the bathrooms. Besides, there is not another room available within fifty miles of Kennebunkport on this snowy night. I am truly sorry that your rooms were not finished in time, but we had so many problems to overcome. I could not get hold of you before you left Connecticut". I had to say something.

We had purchased a live Christmas tree that stayed prostrated on the living floor all during Prelude. I had planned a Christmas decorating party, but our guests had different ideas that weekend that included shopping and town festivities. My eight-year-old niece kept coming to me and telling me, "The stores downtown had things for sale". I didn't relate to what she was referring to until she went home. Hanging on the Christmas tree lying on the floor were her toys tied to the branches!

I was surprised to find out that one of those couples wanted to see some real estate with the idea of opening a bed and breakfast! I knew of one particular property a few blocks over from my own inn that just came on the market for sale. They purchased the property with a warning from me that the town fathers were going to put forth a proposal that only two rooms could be rented in The Village Residential Zone and maybe that proposal could be passed in March. Their reply to me was, " We will have no problems with a zoning change". Their closing was in late March, after the zoning change came effective. The couple created six bedrooms in the main house and then converted their barn into their own living space on the property. I don't know how they did all those renovations

4 ANTICIPATION

On one bright cool summer's day, we retrieved a letter from the post office announcing the travel plans of the British painter, Art, who was going to visit with us. With utter delight, we spirited him to Maine from Logan Airport to become our guest and friend. His charisma swept us up. We lavished him with the best of American food and accommodation. It was our pleasure to share all we had with this proper British icon. We took him all over New England as well as Washington D. C., the Maryland coast and New Jersey coast. A business relationship developed with the idea that he would supply art for the walls of the Inn allowing us to sell his marine paintings for him. I made arrangements to become his American agent in order to elevate his status among both art studios and organizations of marine interest. For instance, an application was made to become a member of the Mystic Maritime Museum in Connecticut. This organization along with other benefits supports and sponsors marine art shows in their museum. The prestige of becoming a member eluded our British painter, because the board could not bring itself to admitting an English artist for the first time even though they all thought his "paintings were exceptional quality". However, they did allow a juried selection of his paintings to be displayed in their annual International Marine Art Show. It was my ambition to introduce him to the American art world. This would have given him a popularity that would have supported a price increase that equaled his quality of painting. He would first pencil sketch a scene on paper. Next, he would transfer his scene onto canvas and paint with oil. A normal oil painting would include about three months of research and painting to get the historical details correct. Oil painting was his prime medium, but he also developed a proficiency in watercolor. He told me that he used to go around England and paint watercolors of noted homes for pocket money. I favored his oils. Each time one would arrive from England, I had it professionally framed and proudly hanged in the Inn. We sold some to our guests for a few thousand dollars each.   I got the painter a commission to paint an oil mural above a fireplace in a home that I sold. Art received the sum of six thousand dollars for his painting. My family members decided to give the artist all the money from his sales to encourage him. The artist started to make an impression in the art world. We were invited to display his art at the International Boat Show in New York.

We welcomed the artist each summer to be part of my family. Some times he would show up in Maine with a member of his family to give them an American experience with us. One time he brought over his wife and then another time his daughter.

My family always wanted to be a part of Kennebunkport. We wanted to be accepted by the community not only for all the money spent locally, but also socially for some enjoyment of our beautiful town. Could this be happening now? One day I returned from the post office with an invite to the River Club for a lobster dinner on July 4th. The invitation said that I could invite a friend as well. I just sold a home on the ocean and those people wanted to join the River Club. I was so excited with anticipation and said to my family, "I must be finally accepted, they want me to join the yacht club".

I took the other couple and proceeded over to a table at the River Club that had chairs turned backwards leaning against the table. I turn them around and sat down with my guests for the lobster feast. Some one tapped me on the shoulder and announced that I was sitting in their spot. I replied, "no problem". I found them two chairs and moved over to make room for them. Most of the people in the hall knew me from the real estate business making easy conversation for me that flowed all night. I really had a good time and decided that I should join their club next year when membership is allowed upon board approval.

Another time I went to the post office and received another invitation to the River Club. This time the club was planning a party for young people with entertainment provided by a magician. This was perfect timing, because my brother was coming to Kennebunkport with his family for their vacation. I called the River Club to arrange the purchase of tickets for the event and was promptly told that the invitation was for another Kennebunkport resident member of the club that has a similar last name to mine. The invitation was placed by the post office in the wrong post office box. I quickly put the phone down and gasped for air. I crashed their lobster dinner! I must be the talk of the town. They will never forgive me.

The British artist wanted to do some public relations around town and asked me if I had any ideas for some publicity. At the time I was so busy with the Inn that I could not think of anything, so I suggested that Art should do a painting of George Bush's boat; our most notable resident of Kennebunkport. A few days later I was shown a pencil rendering of a boat not belonging to George Bush. I knew better and sent the British artist to the River Club. I had first hand knowledge of the boat location and mooring. I told the artist to just give the Secret Service guarding the boat at the River Club my name and what you intend to do. "I am sure they will know who I am and remember me." Art commented on how nice they treated him at the River Club. They even offered him refreshment.

Months later a painting came from England. Art sent me an oil painting depicting George Bush's speedboat, "The Fidelity" cruising by the Bush family compound high on the rocky cliffs of Kennebunkport, Maine. On the inauguration day of George Bush as Vice President in January, I took the painting to the Kennebunkport Post Office and had a stamp attached to the back of the painting. The stamp was hand franked denoting the date of the inauguration.

Somehow during that winter, my aunt sent a correspondence to Vice President George Bush and invited him to pick up the painting the next time he was in town. I knew nothing of this letter and the surprises to follow.

As usual, I picked up the British artist at Logan Airport in Boston for his summer visit with us. This time he informed me that he just flew through customs and was taken back when they asked him if his name was such and such. How could they know his name? I made no further inquiry about this, but I thought it was unusual.

The very next day on a quiet Sunday morning my innkeeper came searching for me to tell me that some man wanted to speak to me at our front desk. As soon as that person saw me, the man blurted out, "The Vice President, George Bush will be here in fifteen minutes". I had recently sold a church down the street from my Inn for a conversion to condominiums that resulted in a few local people resenting the idea. The representative of the group who had purchased the church was visiting with me at the Inn that Sunday morning. He understood that he had to leave before the famous guest arrived. I instructed the innkeeper to go down to The Carriage House and arouse my family and the artist as quickly as possible to come to the Inn with the painting. Instead, the innkeeper upon arriving at my home informed my family that the Inn was surrounded with men that had machine guns. "They are going to gun down the representative of the group who purchased the church". Perplexed by the lack of any response from my family, I made a frantic call home and finally got everyone together to greet our Vice President, George Bush and his wife, Barbara. They accepted our hospitality and most graciously met with Art. They asked our artist many questions and were generally interested in his family in England and his background in art. Our artist told them that he was an art lecturer at university level, but worked in a coalmine when he was young. He developed an interest in marine paintings first as a hobby that turned professional when he received a formal education in engineering. This meeting The Vice President was quite a public relations event that surely should boost the British artist's esteem. The painting was handed over with our best wishes, as we flashed picture after picture of the presentation for posterity.

Normally in front of the Inn there are parked cars in a solid line against the sidewalk, but on that special day, somehow there was not a parked car in sight. Those cars were replaced by hundreds of people who appeared from Dock Square to gawk at the arrival of The Vice President in a caravan of black limos escorted with more Secret Service. I was very impressed by the extent and trouble the Secret

Service went to in securing the safely of The Vice President. Art told me that he saw a man way out on his farm on a telegraph pole a few days before he left for America. Art couldn't figure out what the man was up too. The Secret Service even knew that no one was staying at my Inn. All of these insights added up to include the incident experienced by Art when he came through customs at the airport.

A few days after George Bush's visit, a Secret Service person arrived at the Inn bearing gifts for the artist and his family in England. A special thank you note was included for my family and me.

The second Prelude was soon upon us. I realized that most of our guests were the same ones that booked the first Prelude. To my great surprise, they all said they wanted to see what the Inn looked like finished. I decorated a ten-foot tree with lace and babies breath. Lace designs were cut from a lace cloth. Each piece was soaked in white glue that dried stiff. This looked quite elegant with white lights and a white metal cut out star that looked like lace that was purchased from our local Christmas shop. The mantels displayed large solid brass deer with white sparkling branches. The dining room sported a natural pine ceiling swag from each corner to the chandelier that was decorated with white swan cut out china figurines and holly around the chandelier lights. On the outside of the Inn, each window had a window box with a Christmas tree made from a tomato cage turned upside down. I covered the tomato cage with green garland to cover up the metal wire and added plastic non-breakable red colored round bulbs. The creation was finished with white lights and red ribbon bows. All along the fence I intertwined white lights that went from one end of the Inn to the other. I even took pine tree branches and bent the bear part of one branch to form a neck of a swan. I tied a red ribbon bow onto this branch while the remainder of the pine branch was added to other pine needled branches to imitate feathers on a swan. This was placed on top of the sign. This all looked stunning with two fifty-inch green pine wreaths adoring the front of the Inn. Lawn sticks with glass covers that kept real candles burning lead the way along the path from the street to the front porch of the Inn. Spotlights enhanced the whole Inn giving it a warm and welcome glow. Every night one could see the flash of cameras from passer buyers. A picture of the Inn ended up in a Christmas book called, "Twas The Night Before Christmas". A well-known magazine did a feature article about Kennebunkport's Prelude and added pictures of our Inn to our enjoyment and pride. Our Inn had become a landmark in Kennebunkport and a Prelude showcase for seven years.

Every fall I planted a hundred chrysanthemums all along the outside of the fence along the street. This gave a profusion of color from every angle when a car turned the corner. One year the color would be purple, then another year yellow or orange. This scheme complimented the turning leaves. Fall foliage brought the second season of tourists to New England. I always wanted to discover a way of keep the leaves on the trees in order to extend the fall season, but by November all the beauty ended as we all waited for snow and Prelude.

5 OVERWHELMED

My family decided that Art should have his own art gallery to display and sell his paintings. He certainly proved a promising future and a candidate for great expectations. The Grange Hall just outside of Kennebunkport came on the market for sale. A Grange Hall is a gathering place for farmers to put on shows and events. The Arundel Grange Hall was a perfect venue to convert into an art gallery. The building had two floors. The second floor had a large open space with lots of windows and a stage. The whole building needed restoration, especially the tin ceiling that had water coming through. We spent a whole summer and fall with the help from Art restoring and saving the building from the elements. A new roof, new siding, new public restrooms and everything painted white on the inside turned the Grange Hall into a beautiful show place for art.

I expected Art to fill the space with lots of paintings coming from England during the winter. However, I received very few paintings from Art. My family decided to open up the gallery to painters from across America as long as their art passed our inspection. We ended up representing thirty-five American artists with only one that painted marine paintings. The discrepancy between our painter's art and all the other painters was too much to make a cohesive presentation of similar priced art. We let the artists set their prices, while we commanded a few thousand dollars each for

our British artist paintings. I could not mix any
other art with our British painter's art with the
others. Accommodating the best arrangements
left confining all Art's paintings to the first floor.
I wasn't happy with representing other artists
but I had no choice. We had to fill the space
and pay a mortgage. Art made his annual trip
to America and surveyed his paintings hanging
in The Arundel Art Gallery. I believe Art was
too overwhelmed by the attention and money
spent promoting his interest. It was just too
much for him.

I needed to arrange some sort public
relations for our artist and a grand opening for
the gallery in general. George Bush became
our President and rumors were flying that the
press just didn't like the way they were being
received and treated in Kennebunkport. A
business meeting was quickly held to address
that problem, and a discussion took place on
how other Presidents' hometowns overcame

the bad press problem. I decided to take on this challenge. A simple solution just came to me. I wanted to hold a lobster claim bake at the art gallery as a warm welcoming for the press in hopes that they would write good vibes about Kennebunkport and include my art gallery in their writings. The plan included each businessman attending the affair and paying for a lobster dinner for an invited press member or White House media person. The White House approved the claim bake. Invitations were being printed when our local chamber of Commerce decided to intervene and hold a wine party for the press, which mirrored my best efforts to entertain the press. I had to cancel my affair. Most businessmen decided the wine party was sufficient to show the press how welcome they were in our town. My whole plan went up in smoke. I was paralyzed and lost interest in a grand opening. I could not attend the wine party. I was just too embarrassed to show my face in town. How could I explain the cancellation of my lobster feast?

However, a party of sorts did take place at the Inn. A couple wanted to use the Inn for their wedding. We agreed to all their arrangements. We had the wedding ceremony and the reception. The wedding couple gave me money to arrange all the details that included money for flowers. One of my helpers saw someone in my garden and asked me what they were doing? The flower purveyor was picking my flowers for the wedding. I was so shocked that I couldn't say much as the wedding was only minutes away. The flower purveyor placed many vases throughout the public rooms of the Inn with the flowers she picked from my garden. The flowers were full of ants that escaped the vases and went everywhere including up the pants of the wedding guests. It took us days to get rid of them. The wedding cake was ordered to be a white cake. The bride cut the cake and discovered yellow. Did you know that yellow cake in Maine is white cake according to the cake baker? Why would we complain?

One of our more embarrassing incidents occurred when a chambermaid found some lingerie after cleaning a bedroom. We mailed the undergarments to the registered guest's address. I received a phone call from a very upset lady informing me that she was never in Kennebunkport. She wanted me to check the guest register to see if her husband had signed the guest register. I guess we caused a divorce.

Another time a smoke alarm went off in one of our guest's bedrooms. I sent my sister to investigate. She knocked at the door, but no one was forth coming. She took the master key and entered the room to find a man stark naked staring at her and wondering what was up. My apologies, but your smoke alarm is going off. He replied that more than his, "smoke alarm will be going off, if you don't get out of here now".

One morning a guest came and sat down at the dining room table waiting for his breakfast. I served him a blueberry muffin, juice and coffee. He asked me when the eggs were coming? I told him, "The eggs are in the muffin"! We only served a continental breakfast, but on good china, Spode Blue Trade Winds that depicted a different sailing ship on each piece of china.

Speaking of breakfast, one guest wrote a letter to the manager complaining that they arrived in our dining room for breakfast, but no one showed up to serve them. Upon this complaint they suggested that the owner should fire the person responsible for serving the breakfast. This couple were the only souls staying at the Inn at the time. I left their breakfast on the buffet, but they never noticed.

I learned a lesson one day when I let a couple occupy a room early in the afternoon. I was at the front desk attending negotiations for renting another room when noises from the upstairs bedroom filtered their way down to us. I kept talking louder and louder. We started to hear the headboard knocking against the wall, while the ceiling chandelier over the office reception area started to sway back and forth. I didn't know what to say. I did yell, "The Port Gallery Inn is a very fertile place". The couple started to see me turn red in the face as the sound effects increased.

The Inn made the White House travel list as a recommended place to stay. Anytime President Bush planned to be in Kennebunkport, our Inn was considered for booking. My family thought this could boost our business in the off-season. The trouble with this arrangement was if the President had to cancel his plans to be in Kennebunkport, then we would end up high and dry without a room rented. However, we still went along with this scheme and rented all the rooms one February to the government. We were told that we had to send in a request to the government for payment. We were told that it could take up to six months before we saw a check for the rented rooms. This was too long to wait for money. We had to pay a mortgage every month. I made a call to the travel department and got off the list

One of our guests who came from Idaho wrote me a letter offered me quite a sum of money to ship the whole room after her stay with us. She wanted to buy her bedroom and offered me quite a sum of money to ship the whole room west to her home located on one thousand acres of farmland. This bedroom was decorated in pink flowered wall covering from England with pink carpet and pink adornments. Her grandson chauffeured her all around

America for a final farewell visit before she got too old to travel. I use to play the piano for her in the evenings while her grandson took a break and walked around our town. I didn't send her the room, but she sent me all of her Christmas tree decorations along with a box of Idaho potatoes. I treasure her decorations to this day and put all of them on my tree with the eight hundred and fifty other family ornaments.

One of our guests and his family prepared a full course traditional Mexican dinner in our kitchen at the Inn and served it to my family. This was a complete surprise and unforgettable kindness awarded to us.

One morning all of our guests showed up in the dining room at the same time for their continental breakfast. They heard that a famous T. V. actor was staying at the Inn. My uncle didn't know that he was seated at the table. My uncle started to tease the guests. "He is no better than any of you, and you all came clamoring in here at the same time this morning to see him, but you all missed him, because he left early this morning." I tried kicking my uncle to stop hi m from talking but I was too late. My uncle put his foot in his mouth. The T.V. actor took his remarks on the chin as the room fell silent in shock.

Mainers have a peculiar humor. A car. approaches me and the driver asks, "How do I get to the beach?" I give him directions. I see the same car coming back to me and the driver asks me why did I tell directions that sent him back to me? I replied, "I wanted to find out if you could follow directions first, before I told you how to get to the beach! I don't want to waste my time."

Another car stops me, and the driver asks, "Do you know how to get to the Bush compound"? "Yes I do"(as I walk away).

.

6 CALAMITY

The whole family except for me went off to England for a winter holiday. Yes, this was going to be the quiet time for seaside tourists to venture into New England. We had no mountains for winter sports. However, we did have President's weekend in February. This three-day holiday filled every available room in town. I was stuck alone and had to manage all the daily tasks of running an Inn and cleaning rooms. I was up late one cold clear night and noticed a lot of white smoke escaping out the chimney of The Carriage House. I grabbed my coat and ran down to investigate. I opened the side door of The Carriage House and heard running water. I was afraid to turn on a light for the fear of being electrocuted. A lot of steam hit my face, when I opened the basement door. I could not understand why running water was coming down the ceilings and walls of the house while steam was coming up the basement stairs. Confused and bewildered, I phoned the police for help. They referred me to the fire department. Neither the fire department nor the police would come to my aid. They told me that I needed a plumber. This was now about 2 a.m. in the morning. How was I going to find a plumber? The telephone operator upon my request stayed with me until she finally summoned help from a plumber who answered their phone. The plumber told me how to stop the water going into the house by turning off the main water valve in the street.

The next day I solved my confusion, I found that the water was coming from the third floor. There was an unheated bathroom with a shower stall in the third floor attic area of the house. My uncle overlooked turning off the water and draining the fixtures to winterize that bathroom before going on his holiday to England. Those water pipes in the attic froze and sometime thawed when the sun heated up the temperature of those water pipes during the daytime. I guess the burst pipes with the water gushing out of them went on for hours until I saw all the steam generated from the water dripping onto the hot furnace in the basement.

I knew my job was to save the house and any precious items from water damage. I don't know where the strength came from, but I moved a baby grand piano out of the way from the dripping ceiling covering it with plastic sheets. I took all the oriental rugs and spread them out on the courtyard to dry. A false ceiling in the dining room caved in and exposed a beautiful tin ceiling underneath. Three bedroom ceilings gave way. All the hardwood floors curled up like ripples or waves in an ocean on the first floor of the house. It was a miracle that when the wood dried all the floorboards went back in place like nothing had ever happened. I left the heat on in the house to dry up the moisture, but I kept hearing a funny noise coming from the basement. I ran down the basement stairs to discover a flame shooting about three feet across the area. The interaction of the water dripping onto the furnace and the hot metal finally ate a hole right threw the furnace chamber. The Carriage House could have caught fire. I wonder if the fire department would have come? All and all the estimated damage for insurance purposes came in around thirty-five thousand dollars. The insurance company would not pay for a new or repaired furnace. They insisted water drippings could not have caused any damage to the furnace. They insisted the furnace was old and needed to be replaced at our expense. The furnace was the only mechanical item that worked when we purchased the house!

I told my family to go to the Inn on their return from their holiday. I would explain later. It took a very considerate effort to get our lives back to normal after this calamity. There was an oil shortage and an ongoing crises the same year as our calamity, so we decided to purchase a coal-loading furnace along with a new oil-burning furnace. According to my uncle, the idea was to save money by burning bituminous coal instead of oil. A problem soon surfaced as to where we could purchase such coal that was banned for home heating in New

England. We found a place that sold coal to ships in the next town, Bidderford. We hauled seventy-five pound bags to Kennebunkport. We put the coal into the furnace, but the only thing that heated up was the furnace. Absolutely no heat went to the water pipes that were supposed to circulate and heat the upstairs rooms. My uncle studied this newest calamity for months.   No solution was ever found. Did he install the furnace wrong? We never used this furnace.   I insisted that the professionals who sold us the oil furnace install that one for us.

The only good news was that the water was clean that spilled out of the busted pipes. We did not have to deal with mud. We only needed to dry out the house and remove the damage. I could only save one small piece of wallpaper from the entrance hall of The Carriage House. Thinking it may be worthwhile, I sent it to a museum in Boston to see if they would like to add it to their collections of Colonial Revival Interiors. This wallpaper was hand painted probably in France. A stone home is depicted along with a small pond and trees painted in two degrees of black and gray with a light tint of blue sky. This scene is in dimension like a cut out every so often down the paper. A lighter gray surrounds the cut outs with pictures of musical instruments heading the space between the scenes. The museum sent the piece back to me and declared that they were not interested in the wallpaper for their collection. I became less than enthusiastic to keep any of the other wall coverings in The Carriage House. I stripped and trashed all the other rooms and replaced the wallpaper with ones that my family picked out from common pattern books.

Again, The Carriage House was restored by hiring the local talent who could not even come around a corner in a room with wallpaper the correct way. I thought you cut the wallpaper in a corner after making sure you go down a straight line on the next wall. Those locals said, "Hang lots of pictures and no one will notice. This is how we do it in Maine". The walls were so cracked and rough that wallpapering them did hide a lot of faults, especially doors to no where and windows boarded up. Wallpapering the ceilings presented new challenges. It was worth the effort to do the ceilings because wallpapering prevented the horsehair plaster from falling down. Wallpapered ceilings also covered up the blistering and peeling paint. Little by little The Carriage House came back to life.

The discovery of the tin ceiling in the dining room turn out magnificent once restored and painted. I guess that the back rooms including the dining room and the den room with a tin ceiling comprised the oldest rooms in the house. The two front rooms made two living rooms or front parlor rooms with pocket pulling doors between them along with two upper bedrooms could have been added, filling the space towards the street, leaving only five feet to the road? The two bedrooms located above the dining room and den had a door adjoining the two rooms. This area also had a small baby room connected to one of the bedrooms that went out to the bathroom from the hall. From this second level of the house, stairs rose to a huge attic with a pitched twenty-foot clearance to the top of the roof. This great space could sleep ten people. This space was unfinished and had natural wooded walls and flooring with large beams supporting the whole with only two windows, one at each end of the space. Maybe the house was raised from a single level cottage (now the second floor) and all the first floor rooms were added along with the attic covering the whole house? Someone told us that the house next door was at one time connected to The Carriage House and was used as the kitchen or bake house. Too bad there are no documents or testimonials that come with the purchase of these old homes. We also were told that there was a murder in the house. A sister-in-law had knifed to death a brother-in-law in the kitchen.

One day a roofer inspected the chimneys and found an old tombstone being used as a chimney cap. We also learned that our original owner's son built a house next door to The Carriage House on the south side. This house was taken down some years before we purchased The Carriage House.   The property is now occupied by the telephone company and is used as a sub station.

7 QUANDARY

One winter day in January, just as my family and myself return from our holiday in England a letter was waiting for us at the post office. This letter plainly stated that the town fathers saw more than two car tracks in the snow at the Inn. They insisted that more than two cars were parked in my lot. Please come to the planning board and prove that you are not in violation of the Village Residential Zone and renting more than two rooms. This accusation was forth coming just shy of seven years, the statue of limitations for zoning violations. The violation would have disappeared in March?

No attorney would represent our case. They all cried out that you couldn't fight town hall. I thought that the town was infringing on my Bill of Rights. Can you tell a car manufacturer that they can only make two cars? I was grand fathered and open before the zoning law passed. I could prove this by presenting room reservations, cancelled checks and testimonials. I even sold a property to people that stayed at my Inn, who converted their property to an Inn. All my pleas went unheard. The town fathers told me that I was the issue. They did not care that those people sold their property and turned a good profit when that owner came down with cancer. They would not hear about any other property. The town fathers turned against my family and me.

The said that we should have known that the zoning law was going to pass. They called me a conniving and criminal person who turned a blind-eye to what the town's voters envisioned for the future use of the Village Residential Zone. I should have known better since I was in the real estate business. The town fathers showed me a petition that was circulated secretly around our town that contained some fifty-six signatures of neighbors and businesses all protesting me renting more than two rooms. One of the signatures was from another Inn owner that was located in a commercial zone located across the street from The Carriage House. My reply to the town fathers, after they issued me my ultimatum to rent only two rooms was that they had no idea the devastation this was going to cause my family and me.

The town fathers did not fine me for my violation. They got onto the issue that we had no permit to add bathrooms to the building.

This was just an innocent oversight during the rush to get the Inn open for business for the second town Prelude. They could have insisted that the bathrooms had to be removed. During the middle of that entire trauma, I received another blow. A lawsuit was instigated against me for three hundred thousand dollars in damages.

I sold the bed and breakfast that my sign carver owned to guests that stayed at my Inn. The sign carver had passed away of a heart attack so his wife put the bed and breakfast up for sale. The sign carver only had a building permit to add a garage onto his property. When I showed the property to my guests with the listing agent, the permit was displayed. The unfinished garage area was huge with two stories. The bed and breakfast was purchased, and my new owners immediately made living quarters and bedrooms out of the garage. The new owners even carved out a public restaurant to my surprise. They did all that conversion without consulting the town's building inspector or getting the correct permits for plumbing, electrical or structural. The new owners were in the local newspaper every issue along with me being one of the culprits who sold them the bed and breakfast leading them astray. The real estate agents involved in the sale had a duty to inform what the new owners could do and not do with the property, according to the paper's editorial.

I was advised to get a lawyer who specialized in criminal law. I was running around with my head off until I went to the lawyer who represented the other real estate office who listed the property for sale. He informed me that the party suing me was indeed the listing real estate firm and not my buyers. I took matters in my own hand and asked the other real estate firm to drop all charges against me. After all, I was on their side. I supported the truth and saw a permit for a garage not another addition for living quarters. Somehow that permit disappeared after the property was sold. The town lost their copy of the permit that was issued to the seller some years ago. The wife of my sign carver passed away and the law case followed down into the hands of their kids. The listing real estate firm saw the light and dropped their case against me. My new owners followed suit and dropped their case against the listing firm. The whole mess evaporated into thin air for me. However, the town fathers fined my owners thirty thousand dollars and insisted that they return the property to its original condition. They had to rip out all the improvements and make a garage out of the new addition. My owners got a divorce and sold the bed and breakfast.

My own situation spelled the end of my real estate office from all the bad publicity and press. This also spelled the end of the Inn. There was no way renting two bedrooms would pay for a mortgage. My family made the decision to auction off the premise with all its contents. We could use the art gallery with the stage to show case the contents.   The timing would be perfect. The auction would be during Prelude at The Port Arundel Art Gallery.

Several auctioneers were suggested to us. Most wanted to get inside my home to feast their eyes on personal precious possessions. I grew suspicious of them. A few weeks before the auction event, the weathervane on top of The Carriage House Cupola went missing. I found my ladders hosted up the side of the house and onto the slope of the roof towards the cupola. The weathervane was made from copper forming a three-mast sailing ship. My insurance company accused me of taking the weathervane. They would not compensate me for the loss. It made little difference when we heard that more weathervanes were heisted from mansions along the Kennebunk River.

Our auctioneer was chosen. He suggested that we needed a few more items to spice up the auction. We let him in The Carriage House. He twisted our arm and more items ended up in the art gallery for sale. Just before the auction, the auctioneer insisted that my family sign an agreement that we would not attend the auction. We therefore could not buy back or bid up any items that were selling too low. He would not let us put a reserve price on anything. They call this an absolute auction. The auctioneer sells all items no matter what price they bring. He can't use his discretion to pass over any items he thinks is not bring a reasonable price. He must accept all bids. I wanted to protect myself a little. My brother in Pittsburgh was too busy to attend the auction, but he offered to send his doctor friend to the auction. I only had to tell him what items were the most valuable so he could bid on them.

The day before the auction, Kennebunkport was hit by a twelve plus inch snowstorm. I wanted to call off the auction of the contents, but the auctioneer refused my offer to pay him his twenty percent of the total appraised value of the items. He even refused to auction off the contents on another day. Very few people braved the snow and came to the auction. Most of the people that showed up were just curious seekers. The Inn was auctioned off in the morning and the contents were offered for auction in the afternoon. The doctor friend purchased back a few precious possessions.

The bank that held the mortgage on the art gallery called me to inform me that they could prevent the sale of the Inn unless they received any left over money once the mortgage on the Inn was satisfied. The bank holding the note on the art gallery attended the closing of the Inn and left with the excess money. This money only reduced the number of years left to pay on the art gallery mortgage.

My family sold as estimated one hundred thirty thousand dollars worth of American and English antiques for thirty thousand dollars. This was the total amount of items sold minus another twenty percent auctioneer commission. My brother called from Pittsburgh and instructed us to ship to Pittsburgh all the items purchased by his doctor friend: signed Oriental rug, grandfather clock form England, collection of twenty cut glass and sterling silver perfume bottles, signed Tiffany art glass lamp shade and base and another art glass shade. You must understand my brother said, "The doc paid for those items so he now owns them and should have them. The doctor has made arrangements to have them packed and shipped to Pittsburgh."

After our quandary we decided to take leave of Kennebunkport and travel to England to avoid mental breakdowns and town undercurrents. My family put the art gallery building up for sale. During our sojourn to England, a letter arrived from our insurance company stating that we had abandoned our home and must return to occupy the house or they would drop our insurance. We were running out of money anyhow, so we returned to Kennebunkport. Our bank that held the mortgage on the art gallery declared that we had lost our income when the Inn was sold and real estate office closed. They escalated our mortgage and called in the note to be paid in full within ninety days or they would institute foreclosure proceedings against us.

My family could not keep up with the mortgage payments for the art gallery. I asked my brother to assume that responsibility until the building sold. He reneged and sided with the town and expressed his opinion that I was totally at fault for challenging the zoning laws of Kennebunkport. The bank decided to start foreclosure proceedings against my family when the mortgage payments went dry. One day the president of the bank came calling at The Carriage House to look at "his asset" in the event the art gallery would sell short on the auction block. I asked him if the art gallery sold for less than what I owned the bank would I have the opportunity to secure a mortgage on The Carriage House to cover any minuses. "No, we will sell the art gallery first. If there is any short fall, we are going to sell off you home next, right away. You will not have any time to secure any financing on your home. That is the way it is going to be."

The appraiser for the bank was taking his notes at the art gallery one day and asked me if I was in trouble with the bank. He knew of a person of interest that maybe wanted the art gallery. That person made an offer to purchase the building less than I owned the bank. I took the offer, knowing that I now had time to secure a mortgage on The Carriage House and pay off the bank once and for all. Real estate usually would close forty-five days after an agreement of sale.

My idea backfired due to no income that I could report. Instead, I used my brother's good credit and up dated his tax return to apply for a small loan. I never in the process of obtaining a loan told my brother what I was doing for him. The bank only approved the loan up to a certain amount that was just short of what I needed. I pleaded on behalf of my brother to have the loan increased by only five thousand dollars. I showed up on the doorstep of the bank every day for weeks trying to negotiate an increase. Why was the bank doing this to me? Some times I cried. I finally got my wish, but the loan officer had a massive heart attack the next day on the golf course. My brother only knew about the loan when the bill arrived for a mortgage payment. He did call me to find out what the bill was all about. I told him if he wanted to see his extended family in the street then just ignore the mortgage payment. Too bad my brother refused to support the art gallery until it could have been sold at a breakeven price.

8 A COMFORTLESS HOUSE

Our family "friend" and jewelry storeowner in Kittery, Maine knowing that I may have wanted to get out of town and away from the "fall into disgrace" with no income offered me a salesman job in his shop. This lasted for eight years until The Carriage House sold. I traveled twenty-five miles one way each day to work in his jewelry outlet store for the minimum wage. He expected me to call him if I was going to be late for work. I often wondered where I could find a public phone along my journey on Route 1 to

Kittery, Maine? How could I calculate my arrival time driving through sleet, rain, snow, or behind tourists? He never got real and I never caved into him.

My qualifications for this position selling jewelry in Kittery came from my own family jewelry store that was opened in Pittsburgh, Pennsylvania in a train station turned into a mall. My jewelry store was only open for one year when five men entered and put a knife to my sister's throat and ransacked the jewelry cases. The day before the robbery someone cracked the glass on top of a jewelry case. I was out of town when this happened, but I called a glass company to come over to the store and replace the glass. My uncle thought he could save a few dollars by fetching the glass himself. This left only my sister alone in the jewelry store when those evil men arrived. This sister was the one who developed the cancer. All during her treatment the doctors asked if she ever experienced any trauma. She never mentioned the robbery until she was on her deathbed, telling me how sorry she felt about the robbery.

The mall owners were going to sue me for all the four years rent for closing up shop. I countered with a threat to sue them for not providing security that the merchants were paying for in the lease. The mall owners claimed that the maintenance workers were the security. My loss and the rent I owed for the four years came out about the same. This ended in a standoff. I fled to our home in Ocean City, New Jersey and got the graveyard job at The Golden Nugget Casino in Atlantic City in their coin

department to forget the Pittsburgh
debacle.

Kittery, Maine became a shopping hub for
outlet brand named offerings at a discounted
price. More people went shopping on their
vacations than went to the beaches in Maine.
Shopping became the number one activity for
tourists to do. Shopping tour buses by the
dozens would find their way into the parking
representing any designer names at lots. The
jewelry store wasn't really discount prices. The
owner knew for years the mall developer who
let him have a store. Along with the throngs of
people looking for a bargain, the stores
attracted organized looting gypsies who would
take thousands of dollars in merchandise from
the vulnerable stores who had too few sales
personnel managing the shops.

The Carriage House became a white
elephant. I had given up my business use as a
real estate office for more than two years;

therefore I lost the privilege of that use. This prevented me from selling that use as part of a sales appeal. Anyone purchasing the property would have to ask the town for their own permitted use. However, I always rented a few bedrooms at The Carriage House when the Inn was booked. I needed an official change of use from the town fathers permitting the renting of two rooms, so that I could advertise The Carriage House as a bed and breakfast for sale.

I faced the town fathers again with an array of evidence to convince them that I had always rented rooms at The Carriage House. I had cancelled checks, registration book with all the addresses of people who stayed there. Nothing swayed the town fathers towards letting me continue to rent any rooms or to advertise The Carriage House as a bed and breakfast to attract a buyer. They insisted that I never rented any rooms ever at The Carriage House. I flatly lost my claim.

I went as far as getting a few hundred signatures of voters to change the zoning of my house from Village Residential limited use to Commercial Zone. The question was put on the ballot. Kennebunkport had changed a great deal once we became a stopping point for fifty buses a day to see the town that our President of The United States claimed as his "Summer White House". Those fifty buses were stopping right outside of my front door from morning to night. Most of those people coming off the buses were looking for a restroom and headed towards my door. The voters turned down my proposal to rezone my area on Election Day.

Right across the street from The Carriage House there are a group of six stores all located safely in a commercial zone. One of those stores was rented to a person who turned it into a deli selling what deli's sell including beer. This place of business was open until 2 a.m. There was no parking for cars on the street. A traffic jam sometimes occurred with cars screeching breaks dropping off young people who either sat on the benches outside and talked or entered the establishment slamming a screen door. The local police informed me that there was an obscure curfew for young people twenty and under at midnight. The hours an establishment keeps is their business and no restrictions can be applied. Animosity grew and grew each day as the deli owner found out that I was trying to pressurize the police to enforce the crew few. Was the deli owner selling beer to underage teenagers?

I started to find burnt matches around the trained vine covering the front of the barn over the entrance door. My wooden house and barn was a tinderbox of dry wood. The patrons of the deli started to resent me as word got around town that I was on a warpath. I had to stay up late every night to protect my home from possible harm.

One day with my family members in my van, we heard funny knocking noises coming from under the vehicle just as we pulled out of our courtyard. I pulled over to investigate the matter and found a lighted cigarette attached to string that connected to many little round caps. I drove to the police station to show an officer our predicament. The police officer took pictures and removed all the attachments so we could be on are way. Later that day a police officer came by The Carriage House and informed us that the station master contacted the State Fire Marshall. Their conclusion was to treat this episode as a bomb. They also informed us, The State Attorney's Office will be involved. Therefore, we did not have to become personally involved in the proceedings of this case.

We found out that the deli owner persuaded a sixteen-year-old boy to do the wiring for the firecrackers under my van. The deli was closed, when the owner of the business was arrested. He faced felony charges against him from the State of Maine.

The property owner promised me that in the future he would not rent his store to any food concessions. Peace returned to Spring Street.

The Carriage House had a few interested parties in pursuing the purchase of the property. One party went as far as having a structural inspection done. The inspection revealed rotting sills in the main house. However, the barn was structurally sound. The inspector suggested tearing down the house and then convert the barn to living space. He pointed out the advantage of all the parking we could create. We could save the sixty thousand dollars in estimated costs to lift up the house and replace the dry rotted wooden sills resting on the granite foundation. My family thought his scheme was crazy. Once a property defect is revealed, the defect has to be made aware to all future interested parties. We took the easy way out and reduced our asking price to compensate for the defect.

My family still could not understand why The Carriage House sat for eight years looking for a buyer. I decided to clean out the second floor of the barn. Everything was just stored in the space from unused bathroom fixtures to tons of junk that we collected over twenty-five years. I got the biggest bin available and filled it to the brim. Now anyone who looks at the barn will be able to see the barn with its beautiful wide pine floors and two-story high ceiling to the cupola. Some former owner, who repaired fishing net by hanging it from the high rafters, so we were told, cut out a part of the third story floor. Inside steps to the cupola were left intact from the second floor of the barn.

As soon as I finished this task, The Carriage House was sold.

My aunt had a postcard with a picture of starving concentration camp prisoners in their pinstriped uniforms being freed when the American solders arrived in Germany. "Free At Last". She mailed this postcard to the town fathers.

We arrived in Maine with fifteen truckloads of accumulated family possessions. We left Maine with one along with to many "heartbreaks". When we started the truck engine to pull away from The Carriage House for the last time, one neighbor broke down and cried about the way the town treated us. This neighbor was the mother of the boy who killed himself. As we crossed the bridge over the Kennebunk River, I glazed at the sign with a tear falling down my face: "Leaving Kennebunkport".

DETAILS

Collect all three questionnaires (One from
each of three books) and mail them in
together to see if you answered the
questions correctly. If you answered
them all correctly your name will be
entered into our contest to:
 WIN MY FAMILY HOME.
Winner must legally be able to own real estate
in the U. S. A.
Home Owners Association of Huntington Hills
must accept winner.
Winner will receive a General Warranty Deed.
Deed will pass on or before 30 days after
contest ends.
Winner will be from a random draw of correct
answers to the questions from the three books.

Chances of wining will depend on how many correct entries are received.

Contest ends on or around March 15, 2012

This contest is null and void where it is deemed illegal by any laws to enter such contests. Any minor or underage person who enters shall be considered as null and void entries. Winner will have to pay property taxes, Home Owners Association Dues, Comply with Home Owners Association By-Laws. Title search and Insurance may be done at winner's expense. The winner for the exchange of deed must provide consideration of $1.00. Closing to be agreed upon by winner and owner. Winner will be notified by U. S. mail.

Send you Answer Sheets to:

Francis Edwards

3111 Orange Grove Court

Lakeland, Florida, 33810

No purchase is necessary to enter contest:
Just send me a postcard with your name and
address to the above address and I will send
you the questions sheets.

Visit my Home Web site to see pictures of the properties: You can also order books on my web site:

http://tattletaletalk.webs.com/.

Order ebook:

http://www.smashwords.com/profile/

view/tattletaletalk

QUESTIONS:

Circle the Correct Answer (s)

1.What was the attitude of the author?

Impartial   Downtrodden   Optimistic
Resentful

2. Who raised the author from a child?

Grandmother   Aunt   Uncle   All of them

3. What did the insurance company refuse to pay for?

Weathervane   Furnace   Baby Grand Piano

4. What is the business area of Kennebunkport referred to?

Downtown   Dock Square   Maine Street

5. Who came to the author's aid when the water was pouring down inside The Carriage House?

Police   Telephone operator   Fire Dept.
Plumber

.6. What did the author use the barn for during his ownership?

   Second Hand Shop   Real Estate Office
Jewelry Shop

7.   According to the author, what finally sold The Carriage House?

Location   Cleaning out the barn   Selling it
as a B & B

8.   What did the author hang out a hotel window in London, England?

Chicken   Turkey   Cloths   Shirt

9. What did the author purchase in Vermont?

Maple Syrup   Plants for the garden   Marble
Bench

10. How did the author get into the River Club?

Invited by a member   Called and wanted to join

Received an invitation with a similar name

ABOUT THE AUTHOR

Francis Edwards graduated from The University of Pittsburgh with a B. A. Degree and just finished getting his Master's Degree in Education. He has always been mainly self-employed; hot dog stand in Ocean City, New Jersey; antiques shop in Ocean City, New Jersey; jewelry shop in Pittsburgh, Pennsylvania; Inn owner; art gallery owner; real estate broker (all in Maine); real estate salesman in Delaware, substitute teacher in Florida, dollar store owner in Florida; and now a writer